SELECTED FROM LONESOME DOVE

*

LARRY McMURTRY

WRITERS' VOICES
New Readers Press

New Readers Press
U.S. Publishing Division of Laubach Literacy International
Box 131, Syracuse, New York 13210-0131

Printed in the United States of America

10 9 8 7 6 5 4 3 2

First printing: May 1992

ISBN 0-929631-58-7

Cover designed by Paul Davis Studio
Interior designed by Jules Perlmutter / Off-Broadway Graphics

Acknowledgments

We gratefully acknowledge the generous support of the following foundations and corporations that made the publication of WRITERS' VOICES and NEW WRITERS' VOICES possible: An anonymous foundation; The Vincent Astor Foundation; Exxon Corporation; Knight Foundation; Scripps Howard Foundation; Uris Brothers Foundation and H.W. Wilson Foundation.

This book could not have been realized without the kind and generous cooperation of the author, Larry McMurtry, and his publisher, Simon & Schuster, Inc. Thanks to Beatrice Hurwitz, Director of Permissions.

Our thanks to Paul Davis Studio and Myrna Davis, Paul Davis, Lisa Mazur, Chalkley Calderwood and Alex Ginns for their inspired design of the covers of these books. Thanks also to Jules Perlmutter for his sensitive design of the interior of this book. Thanks also to AnneLouise Burns for design of maps and diagrams.

Contents

Note to the Reader

*

Lonesome Dove brings the exciting world of the Old West to life for modern readers. It is an adventure story and a romance. It is a tale of friendship and a tale of betrayal. The characters you will meet in the book are colorful, bold and, above all, unforgettable.

Every writer has a special voice. That is why we call our series *Writers' Voices*. We chose *Lonesome Dove* because Larry McMurtry's voice can be clearly heard in his descriptions of the Old West and the people who lived on the frontier. We selected portions of *Lonesome Dove* that show the author at his best. You'll discover some very interesting and unusual characters and learn about their complex relationships. You'll explore the exciting world of the American frontier. You'll see how even a close friendship can be put to the test by the code of the Old West.

Our book has several different chapters in addition to the selections. They provide background information that can help you in understanding the selections. You may choose to read some or all of these chapters before or after reading the selections.

- Reading "About the Selections from *Lonesome Dove*" on page 10 will help you begin thinking about the characters and the setting of the story.
- If you would like more information about the frontier, look at the chapter called "About the Old West" on page 58.
- Many readers enjoy finding out about the person who wrote the book. Sometimes this information will give you more insight into the story. You can find out more about Larry McMurtry in the chapter on page 54.
- You may have seen *Lonesome Dove* on television, or you may have heard about this show. If you would like to learn more about the miniseries of *Lonesome Dove*, turn to page 56.

If you are a new reader, you may want to have this book read aloud to you, perhaps more than once. Even if you are a more experienced reader, you may enjoy hearing it read aloud before reading it silently to yourself.

We encourage you to read *actively*. Here are some things you can do.

Before Reading

- Read the front and back covers of the book, and look at the cover illustration. Ask yourself what you expect the book to be about.
- Think about why you want to read this book. Are you interested in the Old West? Have you always wanted to learn more about cowboys? Did you hear about *Lonesome Dove* from the television miniseries?
- Look at the Contents page. See where you can find a map, a list of characters, a glossary and other information. Decide what you want to read and in what order.

During Reading

- There may be place names, names of characters or slang words that are difficult to read. Keep reading to see if the meaning becomes clear. If it doesn't, ask someone for the word. You can also look at the glossary on page 14, which lists many of the difficult words. Or look up the words in the dictionary.
- Ask yourself questions as you read. For example: Would I have been happy living on the frontier? Would I have left the comfort and

safety of a ranch for a 2,500-mile cattle drive to Montana?

After Reading

- Think about what you have read. Did you identify with Gus and Call? Or did you feel sorry for Jake Spoon? Did the book make you see any of your own experiences in a new light?
- Talk with others about your thoughts.
- Try some of the questions and activities in "Questions for the Reader" on page 49. They are meant to help you discover more about what you have read and how it relates to you.

The editors of *Writers' Voices* hope you will write to us. We want to know your thoughts about our books.

About the Selections from LONESOME DOVE

✲

Larry McMurtry's novel *Lonesome Dove* was published in 1985. *Lonesome Dove* takes place in the Old West in the 1880s. It was a time when cowboys herded cattle, fought Indians and drank in saloons. *Lonesome Dove* takes the traditional idea of the American West of "cowboys and Indians" and gives us a different look at the friendships and hardships of the men and women who lived on the frontier.

The book is named for a dusty little town in Texas called Lonesome Dove. The two main characters are Augustus McCrae and Woodrow F. Call.

Augustus, who is called Gus, is a fierce fighter, a romantic lover of women and a great storyteller. His friend Woodrow, who is sometimes called Captain Call or just plain Call, is a very tough leader with no patience for weakness. The two men were Texas Rangers together. (For more about Texas Rangers, see page 61.) Gus and Woodrow are partners in a cattle ranch outside Lonesome Dove.

They have many men to help them run their cattle ranch. One of the people working and living at the ranch is a brave young cowboy named Newt. Newt knows that his mother was a prostitute, and he thinks that his father might be Jake Spoon, a dashing gambler who left Lonesome Dove when Newt was very young.

At the beginning of the selection, Jake Spoon arrives at the ranch along with Deets, a cowboy from the ranch. Jake is an old friend of Gus's and Captain Call's. Jake has accidentally killed a dentist in Arkansas and is now running from a sheriff named July Johnson. Jake tells Gus and Call about the rich farmland in Montana, which is 2,500 miles from Lonesome Dove. Gus and Captain Call both love adventure, and Jake easily convinces them to leave Lonesome Dove and take their cattle north to Montana.

Most of the book *Lonesome Dove* is a description of the cattle drive that takes the men and their cattle from Texas to Montana. Along the way, the men encounter many hardships. They survive sandstorms, stampedes, bandits, floods and snow. As you will see, the relationships among the men are close and difficult at the same time. Gus and Call, for example, are very different personalities, although they have deep feelings for each other.

Cattle and land were the most precious possessions in the Old West. One of the worst crimes on the frontier was taking cattle or horses that didn't belong to you. Cattle and horse thieves were punished by hanging. When a cowboy caught a thief, he didn't wait for the sheriff to arrive. He hung the thief on the spot. This kind of justice was harsh, but everyone knew the law—the "code of the West"—and they were honor-bound to enforce it.

Lonesome Dove is a beautiful portrait of the American West as it was one hundred years ago. It is also a story about friendship and loyalty.

Perhaps it will make you think about deciding to go on an adventure. Or it may remind you of a difficult choice between honor and friendship.

Cast of Characters

*

Woodrow F. Call ("Captain Call"): A partner with Augustus McCrae in the Hat Creek ranch outside of Lonesome Dove.

Deets: A black cowboy who works for McCrae and Call. On the cattle drive, Deets rides ahead as the scout.

July Johnson: A sheriff from Arkansas. He is hunting Jake Spoon, who killed Johnson's brother, a dentist.

Augustus McCrae ("Gus"): A partner with Woodrow Call in the Hat Creek ranch.

Newt: A young cowboy on the ranch.

Pea Eye: A ranch hand.

Jake Spoon: A gambler and a friend of McCrae and Call.

Dan Suggs: A horse thief and the brother of Eddie and Roy Suggs.

Eddie Suggs: A horse thief.

Roy Suggs: A horse thief.

Glossary

*

Bay: A horse with a reddish-brown coat and a black mane and tail.

Blackfeet: Native Americans of the Great Plains.

Canady: Slang for Canada, the country just to the north of the United States.

Cheyenne (*shy*-an): Native Americans of the Great Plains.

Chousing: Slang for "chasing."

Compañeros: A Spanish word for friends.

Free Cattle: Cattle roaming the Great Plains that are not owned by a rancher.

Gant: Slang for "to ride too hard."

Gelding: A male horse that has been castrated.

Guff: Nonsense.

Posse: A group of men who help a sheriff search for an outlaw.

Scabbard: A large pouch or pocket for holding a gun or sword.

Singletree: A wooden bar that connects a plow to a horse.

Sioux (sue): Native Americans of the Great Plains.

Skeer: Slang for "to scare."

Sourdough: Makes bread or biscuits rise.

MAP OF PLACES MENTIONED IN THE SELECTIONS

CANADA
Rocky Mountains
Milk River
MONTANA
Yellowstone River
Great Plains
Mississippi River
KANSAS
MISSOURI
ARKANSAS
ALABAMA
TEXAS
San Antonio
Fort Smith
Fort Worth

The Quarrel, by Frederic Remington.
Courtesy of the National Cowboy Hall of Fame and Western Heritage Center.

SELECTED FROM

LONESOME DOVE

LARRY McMURTRY

*

The Captain had stepped out on the back porch and was looking north, along the stage road that threaded its way through the brush country toward San Antonio. The road ran straight for a considerable distance before it hit the first gully, and Captain Call had his eyes fixed on it. Far up the road he could see two horsemen coming, but they were so far yet that it was impossible to tell anything about them. At moments, heat waves from the road caused a quavering that made them seem like one horseman.

"Gus, come out here," the Captain said.

Augustus was busy cleaning his plate of

honey, a process that involved several more biscuits.

"I'm eating," he said, though that was obvious.

"Come see who's coming," the Captain said, rather mildly.

"If it's Deets my watch is already set," Augustus said. "Anyway, I don't suppose he's changed clothes, and if I have to see his old black knees sticking out of them old quilts he wears for pants it's apt to spoil my digestion."

"Deets is coming all right," Call said. "The fact is, he ain't by himself."

"Well, the man's always aimed to marry," Augustus said. "I imagine he just finally met up with that dark-complexioned lady I was referring to."

"He ain't met no lady," Call said with a touch of exasperation. "Who he's met is an old friend of ours. If you don't come here and look I'll have to drag you."

Augustus was about through with the biscuits anyway. He had to use a forefinger to capture the absolute last drop of honey, which was just as sweet licked off a finger as it was when eaten on good sourdough biscuits.

"Newt, did you know honey is the world's purest food?" he said, getting up.

Newt had heard enough lectures on the subject to have already forgotten more than most people ever know about the properties of honey. He hurried his plate to the tub, more curious than Mr. Gus about who Deets could have found.

"Yes, sir, I like it myself," he said, to cut short the talk of honey.

Augustus was a step behind the boy, idly licking his forefinger. He glanced up the road to see what Call could be so aroused about. Two riders were coming, the one on the left clearly Deets, on the big white gelding they called Wishbone. The other rider rode a pacing bay; it took but a moment for recognition to strike. The rider seemed to slump a little in the saddle, in the direction of his horse's off side, a tendency peculiar to only one man he knew. Augustus was so startled that he made the mistake of running his sticky fingers through his own hair.

" 'I god, Woodrow," he said. "That there's Jake Spoon."

The name struck Newt like a blow, so much did Jake Spoon mean to him. As a very little boy, when his mother had still been alive, Jake Spoon was the man who came most often to see her. It had begun to be clear to him, as he turned over his memories, that his mother had been a whore, but this realization tarnished nothing, least of all his memories of Jake Spoon. No man had been kinder, either to him or his mother—her name had been Maggie.

But the settled life seemed not to suit Jake, and one day he was just gone. No one was surprised, though Newt's mother was so upset by it that for a time he got a whipping every time he asked when Jake was coming back. The whippings didn't seem to have much to do with him, just with his mother's disappointment that Jake had left.

Newt stopped asking about Jake, but he didn't stop remembering him. It was barely a year later that his mother died of fever; the Captain and Augustus took him in.

It seemed to him that Jake might even be his father, though everyone told him his name was Newt Dobbs, not Newt Spoon. Why it was Dobbs, and why everyone was so sure, was a puzzle to him, since no one in Lonesome Dove seemed to know anything about a Mr. Dobbs. It had not occurred to him to ask his mother while she was alive—last names weren't used much around Lonesome Dove, and he didn't realize that the last name was supposed to come from the father. Even Mr. Gus, who would talk about anything, seemed to have no information about Mr. Dobbs. "He went west when he shouldn't have," was his only comment on the man.

Newt had never asked Captain Call to amplify that information—the Captain preferred to volunteer what he wanted you to know. In his heart, though, Newt didn't believe in Mr. Dobbs. He had a little pile of stuff his mother had left, just a few beads and combs and a little scrapbook and some cutout pictures from magazines that Mr. Gus had been kind enough to save for him, and there was nothing about a Mr. Dobbs in the scrapbook and no picture of him amid the pictures, though there was a scratchy picture of his grandfather, Maggie's father, who had lived in Alabama.

If, as he suspected, there had been no Mr. Dobbs, or if he had just been a gentleman who stopped at the rooming house a day or two—they had lived in the rooming house when Maggie was alive—then it might be that Jake Spoon was really his father. Perhaps no one had informed him of it because they thought it more polite to let Jake do so himself when he came back.

Now the very man was riding toward them, right there beside Deets, on a pacing horse as pretty as the one he had ridden away ten years before. Before the two riders even got very close Newt could see Deets's big white teeth shining in his black face, for he had gone away on a routine job and was coming back proud of more than having done it. He didn't race his horse up to the porch or do anything silly, but it was plain even at a distance that Deets was a happy man.

Then the horses were kicking up little puffs of dust in the wagon yard and the two were almost there. Jake wore a brown vest and a brown hat, and he still had his pearl-handled pistol. Deets was still grinning. They rode right up to the back porch before they drew rein. It was obvious that Jake had come a long way, for the pacing bay had no flesh on him.

Jake's eyes were the color of coffee, and he wore a little mustache. He looked them all over for a moment, and then broke out a slow grin.

"Howdy, boys," he said. "What's for breakfast?"

"Why, biscuits and fatback, Jake," Augustus said. "The usual fare. Only we won't be serving it up for about twenty-four hours. I hope you've got a buffalo liver or a haunch of venison on you to tide you over."

"Gus, don't tell me you've et," Jake said, swinging off the bay. "We rode all night, and Deets couldn't think of nothing to talk about except the taste of them biscuits you make."

"While you was talking, Gus was eating

them," Call said. He and Jake shook hands, looking one another over.

Jake looked at Deets a minute. "I knowed we should have telegraphed from Pickles Gap," he said, then turned with a grin and shook Gus's hand.

"You always was a hog, Gus," Jake said.

"And you were usually late for meals," Augustus reminded him.

While they were shaking Jake noticed the boy, standing there by some lank cowhand with a heavy mustache. "My lord," he said. "Are you little Newt? Why you're plumb growed. Who let that happen?"

Newt felt so full of feeling that he could hardly speak. "It's me, Jake," he said. "I'm still here."

Jake turned and had another look at Newt as if the fact that he was nearly grown surprised him more than anything else in Lonesome Dove.

Jake turned his coffee eyes on Augustus and broke out another slow grin. "What'd it take to get you to whip up another batch of them biscuits?" he said. "I've come all the way from Arkansas without tasting a good bite of bread."

"From the looks of that pony it's been fast traveling," Call said, which was as close to prying as he intended to get. He had run with

Jake Spoon off and on for twenty years, and liked him well; but the man had always worried him a little, underneath. There was no more likable man in the west, and no better rider, either; but riding wasn't everything, and neither was likableness. Something in Jake didn't quite stick. Something wasn't quite consistent. He could be the coolest man in the company in one fight, and in the next be practically worthless.

"Boys, I'd like a drink and maybe even a wash, if you can spare one," he said. "My luck's been running kinda muddy lately, but I'd like to get water enough in me that I can at least spit before I tell you about it."

"Why, sure," Augustus said. "Go fill the dipper. You want us to stay out here and hold off the posses?"

"There ain't no posses," Jake said, going in the house.

Jake stepped out on the back porch, his sleeves rolled up and his face red from the scrubbing he had given it with the old piece of sacking they used for a towel. "What about them biscuits?"

"Much as I've missed you, I ain't overworking my sourdough just because you and Deets couldn't manage to get here in time," Augustus said. "What I will do is fry some meat."

He fried it, and Jake and Deets ate it. It

amused Augustus to watch Jake eat—he was so fastidious about it—but the sight put Call into a black fidget. Jake could spend twenty minutes picking at some eggs and a bit of bacon. It was obvious to Augustus that Call was trying to be polite and let Jake get some food in his belly before he told his story, but Call was not a patient man and had already controlled his urge to get to work longer than was usual. He stood in the door, watching the whitening sky and looking restless enough to bite himself.

"So where have you been, Jake?" Augustus asked, to speed things up.

Jake looked thoughtful, as he almost always did. His coffee-colored eyes always seemed to be traveling leisurely over scenes from his own past, and they gave the impression that he was a man of sorrows—an impression very appealing to the ladies. It disgusted Augustus a little that ladies were so taken in by Jake's big eyes. In fact, Jake Spoon had had a perfectly easy life, doing mostly just what he pleased and keeping his boots clean; what his big eyes concealed was a slow-working brain. Basically Jake just dreamed his way through life and somehow got by with it.

"Oh, I've been seeing the country," he said. "I was up to Montana two years ago. I guess that's what made me decide to come back, although I've been meaning to get back down this way and see you boys for some years."

Call came back in the room and straddled a chair, figuring he might as well hear it.

"What's Montana got to do with us?" he asked.

"Why, Call, you ought to see it," Jake said. "A prettier country never was."

"How far'd you go?" Augustus asked.

"Way up, past the Yellowstone," Jake said. "I was near to the Milk River. You can smell Canady from there."

"I bet you can smell Indians too," Call said. "How'd you get past the Cheyenne?"

"They shipped most of them out," Jake said. "Some of the Blackfeet are still troublesome. But I was with the Army, doing a little scouting."

That hardly made sense. Jake Spoon might scout his way across a card table, but Montana was something else.

"When'd you take to scouting?" Call asked dryly.

"Oh, I was just with a feller taking some beef to the Blackfeet," Jake said. "The Army came along to help."

"A lot of damn help the Army would be, driving beef," Gus said.

"They helped us keep our hair," Jake said, laying his knife and fork across his plate as neatly as if he were eating at a fancy table.

"My main job was to skeer the buffalo out of the way," he said.

"Buffalo," Augustus said. "I thought they was about gone."

"Pshaw," Jake said. "I must have seen fifty thousand up above the Yellowstone. The damn buffalo hunters ain't got the guts to take on them Indians. Oh, they'll finish them, once the Cheyenne and the Sioux finally cave in, and they may have even since I left. The damn Indians have the grass of Montana all to themselves. And has it got grass. Call, you ought to see it."

"I'd go today if I could fly," Call said.

"Be safer to walk," Augustus said. "By the time we walked up there maybe they would have licked the Indians."

"That's just it, boys," Jake said. "The minute they're licked there's going to be fortunes made in Montana. Why, it's cattle land like you've never seen, Call. High grass and plenty of water."

"Chilly, though, ain't it?" Augustus asked.

"Oh, it's got weather," Jake said. "Hell, a man can wear a coat."

"Better yet, a man can stay inside," Augustus said.

"I've yet to see a fortune made inside," Call said. "Except by a banker, and we ain't bankers. What did you have in mind, Jake?"

"Getting to it first," Jake said. "Round up some of these free cattle and take 'em on up. Beat all the other sons of bitches, and we'd soon be rich."

"Jake, if you ain't something," Augustus said. "Here we ain't seen hide nor hair of you for ten years and now you come riding in and want us to pack up and go north to get scalped."

"Well, Gus, me and Call are going bald anyway," Jake said. "You're the only one whose hair they'd want."

"All the more reason not to carry it to a hostile land," Augustus said. "Why don't you just calm down and play cards with me for a few days? Then when I've won all your money we'll talk about going places."

Jake whittled down a match and began to meticulously pick his teeth.

"By the time you clean me, Montana will be all settled up," he said. "I don't clean quick."

"What about that horse?" Call asked. "You didn't gant him like that just so you could get here and help us beat the rush to Montana. What's this about your luck running thick?"

Jake looked a little more sorrowful as he picked his teeth. "Kilt a dentist," he said. "A pure accident, but I kilt him."

"Where'd this happen?" Call asked.

"Fort Smith, Arkansas," Jake said. "Not three weeks ago."

"Well, I've always considered dentistry a dangerous profession," Augustus said. "Making a living by yanking people's teeth out is asking for trouble."

Jake said, "Everybody in town liked that dentist."

"Aw, Jake, that won't stick," Augustus said. "Nobody really likes dentists."

"This one was the mayor," Jake said.

"Well, it was accidental death," Call said.

"Yeah, but I'm just a gambler," Jake said. "They all like to think they're respectable back in Arkansas. Besides, the dentist's brother was the sheriff."

"How'd you get loose from the sheriff?" Call asked.

"He was gone when it happened," Jake said. "He was up in Missouri, testifying on some stage robbers. I don't know if he's even back to Fort Smith yet."

"They wouldn't have hung you for an accident, even in Arkansas," Call said.

"I am a gambler, but that's one I didn't figure to gamble on," Jake said. "I just went out the back door and left, hoping July would get too busy to come after me."

"July's the sheriff?" Gus asked.

"Yes, July Johnson," Jake said. "He's young, but he's determined. I just hope he gets busy."

"I don't know why a lawman would want a dentist for a brother," Augustus said rather absently.

Jake let it pass. Gus would have his joke, and he and Call *would* disapprove of him when he got in some unlucky scrape. It had always been that way. But the three of them were *compañeros* still, no matter how many dentists he killed. Call and Gus had been the law themselves and didn't always bow and scrape to it. They would not likely let some young sheriff take him off to hang because of an accident. He was willing to take a bit of ribbing. When trouble came, if it did, the boys would stick and July Johnson would have to ride back home empty-handed.

"Well, it ain't a holiday," Call said. "Work to do. Me and Deets will go see if we can help them boys."

"That Newt surprised me," Jake said. "I had it

in mind he was still a spud. Is Maggie still here?"

"Maggie's been dead nine years," Augustus said. "You wasn't hardly over the hill when it happened."

"I swear," Jake said. "You mean you've had little Newt for nine years?"

"Why, yes, Jake," Gus said. "We've had him since Maggie died."

"I swear," Jake said again.

"It was only the Christian thing," Augustus said. "Taking him in, I mean. After all, one of you boys is more than likely his pa."

Call put on his hat, picked up his rifle and left them to their talk.

Augustus, Captain Call, Deets and the other cowboys start the long cattle drive from Texas to Montana. Jake Spoon loses interest in the cattle drive along the way and parts company with Gus and Woodrow.

Gus and Woodrow have many adventures on their trip. When they are in Kansas, about halfway from Lonesome Dove to Montana, they find a man named Wilbarger, who has been shot, and his herd of horses has been stolen by the Suggs brothers. Wilbarger dies. Gus, Woodrow and the cowboys discover the bodies of two of

Wilbarger's men who were killed by the Suggs gang: Chick and a young boy.

When they found Wilbarger's man Chick and the boy who had been traveling with them, there wasn't much left to bury. The coyotes and buzzards had had a full day at them.

The smell suddenly got to Newt—he dismounted and was sick. Pea Eye dug a shallow grave with a little shovel they had brought. They rolled the remains in the grave and covered them, while the buzzards watched. Many stood on the prairie, like a black army, while others circled in the sky. Deets went off to study the thieves' tracks. Newt had vomited so hard that he felt lightheaded, but even so, he noticed that Deets didn't look happy when he returned.

"How many are we up against?" Call asked.

"Four," Deets said. "Just four."

"Hell, there's five of us," Augustus said. "There's less than one apiece of the horsethieves, so what are you so down about?"

Deets pointed to a horse track. "Mr. Jake is with them," he said. "That's his track."

They all looked at the track for a moment.

"Well, they're horsethieves and murderers," Augustus reminded them.

The news hit Call hard. He had stopped expecting anything of Jake Spoon, and had supposed they would travel different routes for the rest of their lives. Jake would gamble and whore—he always had. No one expected any better of him, but no one had expected any worse, either. Jake hadn't the nerve to lead a criminal life, in Call's estimation. But there was his track, beside the tracks of three killers.

"Well, I hope you're wrong," he said to Deets.

Deets was silent. So, for once, was Augustus. If Jake was with the killers, then there was no hope for him.

A few hours later they came upon the dead settlers, still hanging, shreds of charred clothes clinging to their bodies. A coyote was tugging at the foot of one of them, trying to pull the body down. It ran when the party approached. Newt wanted to be sick again, but had nothing in his stomach. He had never expected to see anything more awful than the buzzard-torn bodies they had buried that morning, and yet it was still the same day and already there was a worse sight. It seemed the farther they went through the plains, the worse things got.

Call was thinking of Jake—that a man who had ridden with them so long could let such a thing happen. Of course he was outnumbered, but it was no excuse. He could have fought or run, once he saw the caliber of his companions.

Deets had ridden on, to evaluate the trail. They overtook him a few hours later. His face was sad.

"They're close," he said. "Stopped at a creek."

"Probably stopped to baptize one another," Augustus said. "Did you see 'em, or just smell 'em?"

"I seen 'em," Deets said. "Four men."

"What about Jake?" Call asked.

"He's one," Deets said.

"Are they just watering the stock, or have they camped?" Call wanted to know.

"They're camped," Deets said. "They killed somebody in a wagon and he had whiskey."

"More work for the gravediggers," Augustus said, checking his rifle. "We better go challenge them before they wipe out Kansas."

Pea Eye and Newt were left with the horses. Deets led Call and Augustus on foot for a mile. They crept up the crest of a ridge and saw Wilbarger's horses grazing three or four miles away on the rolling prairie. Between them and the horse herd was a steep banked creek. A small wagon was stopped on the near bank, and four men were lounging on their saddle blankets. One of the men was Jake Spoon. The corpse of the man who had been driving the wagon lay some fifty yards away. The men on the blankets were amusing themselves by shooting their pistols at the buzzards that attempted to approach the corpse. One man, annoyed at missing with his pistol, picked up a rifle and knocked over a buzzard.

"They're cocky, I'd say," Call said. "They don't even have a guard."

"Well, they've killed the whole population of this part of the country except us, and we're just wandering through," Augustus said.

"Let's wait awhile," Call said. "When they're good and drunk we'll come along the creek bed and surprise 'em."

They waited until late afternoon, when the sun was angling down toward the horizon. Then, walking a wide circle to the east, they struck the creek a mile below where the men were camped and walked quietly up the creek bed. The banks were high and made a perfect shelter. They saw three horses watering at the creek, and Call feared the animals would give them away, but the horses were not alarmed.

Soon they heard the faint talk of the men—they were still lounging on their saddle blankets.

Call, in the lead, crept a little closer.

"Let's stay the night," he heard a man say.

"I'm too full of liquor to be chousing horses in the dark."

"It'll sober you up," another voice said. "It's cooler traveling at night."

"Why travel?" the first man said. "Some more wagons might come along and we could rob 'em. It's easier than banks."

"Eddie, you're as lazy as Jake," the second voice said. "Neither one of you pulls your weight in this outfit."

"I'd have to be quick to beat you at killing people, Dan," little Eddie said.

Call and Augustus looked at one another. Dan Suggs was the name Wilbarger had mentioned—he had called his killers accurately.

Jake was lying on his saddle blanket feeling drunk and depressed. Dan Suggs had shot the old man driving the wagon at a hundred yards' distance, without even speaking to him. Dan had been hiding in the trees along the creek, so the old man died without even suspecting that he was in danger. He only had about thirty dollars on him, but he had four jugs of whiskey, and they were divided equally, although Dan claimed he ought to have two for doing the shooting. Jake had been drinking steadily, hoping he would get so drunk the Suggses would just go off and leave him. But he knew they wouldn't. For one thing, he had eight hundred dollars on him, won in poker games in Fort Worth, and if Dan Suggs didn't know it, he certainly suspected it. They wouldn't leave him without robbing him, or rob him without killing him, so for the time being his hope was to ride along and not rile Dan.

He had been lying flat down, for he felt very weary, but he raised up on his elbow to take another swig from the jug, and he and little Eddie saw the three men at the same moment: three men with leveled rifles, standing on the riverbank with the sun at a blinding angle right behind them. Jake had taken off his gun belt—he couldn't rest comfortably with it on. Little Eddie had his pistol on and grabbed for it, but a rifle cracked and a bullet took him in the shoulder and kicked him back off the saddle blanket.

Dan and Roy Suggs were sitting with their backs to the creek, each with a jug between their legs. They were caught cold, their rifles propped on their saddles well out of reach.

"Sit still, boys," Call said, as soon as the crack of the shot died. Deets, who had the best angle, had shot little Eddie.

Dan Suggs leaped to his feet and turned to see the bright sun glinting on three rifle barrels.

"Who are you?" he asked. "We're horse traders, so hold your damn fire."

He realized it would be suicide to draw and decided a bluff was his best chance, though the shock, plus the whiskey he had just drunk, made him unsteady for a moment. It was a moment too long, for a black man with a rifle stepped behind him and lifted his pistol. Roy Suggs was sitting where he was, his mouth open, too surprised even to move. Little Eddie lay flat on his back, stunned by his shoulder wound.

Augustus took little Eddie's pistol as he stepped over him, and in a moment had Roy's. Deets got the rifles. Call kept his gun trained right on Dan Suggs, who, because of the sun, still could not see clearly whom he faced.

Deets, with a downcast look, picked up Jake's gun belt.

"Why, Deets, do you think I'd shoot you?" Jake asked, though he knew too well where he stood, and if he had moved quicker would have shot, whatever the cost. A clean bullet was better than a scratchy rope, and his old partners could shoot clean when they wanted to.

Deets, without answering, removed the rifle from Jake's saddle scabbard.

"Get your boots off, boys," Call said, coming closer.

"Goddamned if we will," Dan Suggs said, his

anger rising. "Didn't you hear me? I told you we were horse traders."

"We're more persuaded by that dead fellow over there," Augustus said. "He says you're murderers. And Mr. Wilbarger's good horses says you're horsethieves to boot."

"Just ask Jake if we didn't buy these horses," Dan said. "Jake's a friend of yours, ain't he?"

"Did you buy that old man?" Call asked. "Did you buy them two farmers you burned? Did you buy Wilbarger and his man and that boy?"

Little Eddie sat up. When he saw that his shirt was drenched with blood, his face went white. "I'm bleeding, Dan," he said.

Call went over to Jake. Deets seemed hesitant to tie him, but Call nodded and covered Jake with his rifle while Deets tied his hands. As he was doing it Pea Eye and Newt came over the hill with the horses.

"Call, he don't need to tie me," Jake said. "I ain't done nothing. I just fell in with these boys to get through the Territory. I was aiming to leave them first chance I got."

Call saw that Jake was so drunk he could barely sit up.

"You should have made a chance a little sooner, Jake," Augustus said. "A man that will go along with six killings is making his escape a little slow."

Jake got to his feet awkwardly, for his hands were tied behind him. He looked at Pea Eye, who was standing quietly with Deets.

"Pea, you know me," Jake said. "You know I ain't no killer. Old Deets knows it too. You boys wouldn't want to hang a friend, I hope."

"I've done many a thing I didn't want to do, Jake," Pea Eye said.

Jake walked over to Augustus. "I ain't no criminal, Gus," he said. "Dan's the only one that done anything. He shot that old man over there, and he killed them farmers. He shot Wilbarger and his men. Me and the other boys have killed nobody."

"We'll hang him for the killings and the rest of you for the horse theft, then," Augustus said. "Out in these parts the punishment's the same, as you well know.

"Ride with an outlaw, die with him," he added. "I admit it's a harsh code. But you rode on the other side long enough to know how it works. I'm sorry you crossed the line, though."

Jake's momentary optimism had passed, and he felt tired and despairing. He would have liked a good bed in a whorehouse and a nice night's sleep.

"I never seen no line, Gus," he said. "I was just trying to get to Kansas without getting scalped."

Newt had saddled the men's horses. Call came back and took the ropes off the four saddles.

"We're lucky to have caught 'em by the trees," he said. Newt felt numb from all that he had seen.

"Have we got to hang Jake too?" he asked. "He was my ma's friend."

Call was surprised by the remark. Newt was surprised too—it had just popped out. He remembered how jolly Jake had been, then—it was mainly on Jake's visits that he had heard his mother laugh. It puzzled him how the years could have moved so, to bring them from such happy times to the moment at hand.

"Yes, he's guilty with the rest of them," Call said. "Any judge would hang him."

He walked on, and Newt put his cheek for a moment against the warm neck of the horse he had just saddled. The warmth made him want to cry. His mother had been warm too, in the years when they first knew Jake. But he couldn't bring any of it back, and Jake was standing not twenty yards away, weaving from drink, his hands tied, sad-looking. Newt choked back his feelings and led the horses over.

The men had to be helped onto the horses because of the way their hands were tied. Little Eddie had lost a lot of blood and was so weak he could barely keep his seat.

"I'll lead yours, Jake," Newt said, hoping Jake would realize he meant it as a friendly gesture. Jake had several days' stubble on his face and looked dirty and tired; his eyes had a dull look in them, as if he merely wanted to go to sleep.

Call took the rein of Dan Suggs's horse, just in case Dan tried something—though there was little he could try. Augustus walked behind and Pea Eye led the other two horses. Deets went ahead to fix the nooses—he was good with knots. Call kept the horse under tight control and in no time they came to the tree with the four dangling nooses.

It took a while for Deets to fix the knots to his satisfaction. The twilight began to deepen into dusk.

Jake tried to get his mind to work, but it wouldn't snap to. He had the feeling that there ought to be something he could say that would move Call or Gus on his behalf. It made him proud that the two of them had caught Dan Suggs so easily, although it had brought him to a hard fix. Still, it cut Dan Suggs down to size. Jake tried to think back over his years of rangering—to try and think of a debt he could call in, or a memory that might move the boys—but his brain seemed to be asleep. He could think of nothing. The only one who seemed to care was the boy Newt—Maggie's boy, Jake remembered. She had fat legs, but she was always friendly, Maggie. Of all the whores he had known, she was the easiest to get along with. The thought crossed his mind that he ought to have married her and not gone rambling. If he had, he wouldn't be in such a fix. But he felt little fear; just an overpowering fatigue. Life had slipped out of line. It was unfair, it was too bad, but he couldn't find the energy to fight it any longer.

Deets finally got the nooses done. He mounted and rode behind each man, to carefully set the knots. Little Eddie submitted quietly, but Dan Suggs shook his head and struggled like a wildcat when Deets came to him.

"Nigger boy, don't you get near me," he said. "I won't be hung by no black nigger."

Call and Augustus had to grab his arms and hold him steady. Dan dug his chin into his chest, so that Deets had to grab his hair and pull his head back to get the rope around his neck.

"You're a fool, Suggs," Augustus said. "You don't appreciate a professional when you see one. Men Deets hangs don't have to dance on the rope, like some I've seen."

"You're yellowbellies, both of you, or you would have fought me fair," Dan Suggs said, glaring down at him. "I'll fight you yet, bare-handed, if you'll just let me down. I'll fight the both of you right now, and this nigger boy too."

"You'd do better to say goodbye to your brothers," Call said. "I expect you got them into this."

"They're not worth a red piss and neither are you," Dan said.

"I'll say this for you, Suggs, you're the kind of son of a bitch it's a pleasure to hang," Augustus said. "If guff's all you can talk, go talk it to the devil."

He gave Dan Suggs's horse a whack with a coiled rope and the horse jumped out from under him. When Dan's horse jumped, little Eddie's bolted too, and in a moment the two men were both swinging dead from the limb.

"It's damn bad luck, having a big brother like Dan Suggs, I'd say," Augustus said.

He walked over to Jake and put a hand on his leg for a moment.

Call walked over. Now that they were about it he felt a keen sorrow. Jake had ridden the river with them and been the life of the camp once—

not the steadiest boy in the troop, but lively and friendly to a fault.

"Well, it'll soon be dark," he said. "I'm sorry it's us, Jake—I wish it had fallen to somebody else."

Jake grinned. Something in the way Call said it amused him, and for a second he regained a bit of his old dash.

"Hell, don't worry about it, boys," he said. "I'd a damn sight rather be hung by my friends than by a bunch of strangers. The thing is, I never meant no harm," he added. "I didn't know they was such a gun outfit."

He looked down at Pea Eye and Deets, and at the boy. Everyone was silent, even Gus, who held the coiled rope. They were all looking at him, but it seemed no one could speak. For a moment, Jake felt good. He was back with his old *compañeros*, at least—those boys who had haunted his dreams. Straying off from them had been his worst mistake.

"Well, *adiós*, boys," he said. "I hope you won't hold it against me."

He waited a moment, but Augustus seemed dumbstruck, holding the rope.

Jake looked down again and saw the glint of tears in the boy's eyes. Little Newt cared for him, at least.

"Newt, why don't you take this pony?" he said, looking at the boy. "He's a pacer—you won't find no easier gait. And the rest of you boys divide what money's in my pocket."

He smiled at the thought of how surprised they would be when they saw how much he had—it was that lucky week in Fort Worth he had to thank for it.

"All right, Jake, many thanks," Newt said, his voice cracking.

Before he got the thanks out, Jake Spoon had quickly spurred his pacing horse high back in the flanks with both spurs. The rope squeaked against the bark of the limb. Augustus stepped over and caught the swinging body and held it still.

"I swear," Pea Eye said. "He didn't wait for you, Gus."

"Nope, he died fine," Augustus said. "Go dig him a grave, will you, Pea?"

They buried Jake Spoon by moonlight on the slope above the creek and, after some discussion, cut down Roy Suggs and little Eddie [and buried them], plus the old man Dan Suggs had killed.

Dan Suggs they left hanging. Augustus took one of the circulars and wrote "Dan Suggs, Man Burner and Horse Thief" on the back of it. He rode over and pinned the sign to Dan Suggs's shirt.

"That way if a lawman comes looking for him he'll know he can quit the search," Augustus said.

They rounded up Wilbarger's horses and unhitched the two mules that had been pulling the little wagon.

Call broke up the tailgate [of the wagon] and made a little marker for Jake's grave, scratching his name on it with a pocketknife by the light of the old man's lantern. He hammered the marker into the loose-packed dirt with the blunt side of a hatchet they had found in the wagon. Augustus trotted over, bringing Call his mare.

"I'm tired of justice, ain't you?" he asked.

"Well, I wish he hadn't got so careless about his company," Call said. "It was that that cost him."

"Life works out peculiar," Augustus said. "If he hadn't talked you into making this trip, we wouldn't have had to hang him today. He could be sitting down in Lonesome Dove, playing cards."

"On the other hand, it was gambling brought him down," Call said. "That's what started it."

Deets and Pea Eye and Newt held the little horse herd. Newt was leading the horse Jake had left him. He didn't know if it was right to get on him so soon after Jake's death.

"You can ride the pacing pony," Deets said. "Mister Jake meant you to have it."

"What will I do with his saddle?" Newt asked. "He didn't say anything about the saddle."

"It's better than that old singletree of yours," Pea Eye said. "Take it—Jake's through with it."

"Don't neither of you want it?" Newt asked. It bothered him to take it, for Jake hadn't mentioned it.

"Oh, no," Deets said. "Saddle goes with the horse, I guess."

Nervous and a little reluctant, Newt got on Jake's horse. The stirrups were too long for him, but Deets got down and quickly adjusted them. As he was finishing the lacing, Call and Augustus rode by. Deets took the bridle off Newt's other horse and turned him, still saddled, into the horse herd. No one seemed to have anything to say.

They started Wilbarger's horses west across the dark prairie in the direction the cattle should be.

Questions for the Reader

Thinking About the Story

1. What was interesting for you about the selections from *Lonesome Dove*?
2. Did the events or people in the selections become important or special to you in some way? What do you think of Jake? Gus? Call? Newt? Did your feelings change as you read the selections? Write about or discuss your answers.
3. What did you think were the most important things Larry McMurtry wanted to say in the selections?
4. In what ways did the selections answer the questions you had before you began reading or listening?
5. Were any parts of the selections difficult to understand? If so, you may want to read or listen to them again. Discuss with your learning partners possible reasons why they were difficult.

Thinking About the Writing

1. How did Larry McMurtry help you see and hear life on the ranch or life on the trail in the selections? Find the words, phrases or sentences that did this best.

2. Writers think carefully about their stories' settings, characters and events. In writing the selections, which of these things do you think Larry McMurtry felt was most important? Find the parts of the story that support your opinion.

3. In the selections, Larry McMurtry uses dialogue. Dialogue can make a story more alive. Besides telling the reader what the characters said, the dialogue helps to bring out the personalities of the characters. Pick out some dialogue that you feel is strong, and explain how it helps the story.

4. The selections from *Lonesome Dove* are written from the point of view of someone outside the story who tells us what is happening. The writer uses the words "he" and "she" rather than "I" or "me." What difference does this create in the writing of the selections?

5. Larry McMurtry, through his writing, makes us feel the sadness of Gus and Woodrow as

they have to hang their old friend Jake. Find some parts in the selections that helped you feel that sadness.

Activities

1. Were there any words that were difficult for you in the selections from *Lonesome Dove*? Go back to these words and try to figure out their meanings. Discuss what you think each word means and why you made that guess. Look them up in a dictionary and see if your definitions are the same or different.

   Discuss with your learning partners how you are going to remember each word. Some ways to remember words are to put them on file cards, write them in a journal or create a personal dictionary. Be sure to use the words in your writing in a way that will help you to remember their meanings.

2. Talking with other people about what you have read can increase your understanding. Discussion can help you organize your thoughts, get new ideas and rethink your original ideas. Discuss your thoughts about the selections from *Lonesome Dove* with someone else who has read them. Find out if you helped yourselves understand the

selections in the same or different ways. Find out if your opinions about the selections are the same or different. See if your thoughts change as a result of this discussion.

3. After you finish reading or listening, you might want to write down your thoughts about the book. You could write your reflections on the book in a journal, or you could write about topics the book has brought up that you want to explore further. You could write a book review or a letter to a friend you think might be interested in the book.

4. Did reading the selections give you any ideas for your own writing? You might want to write about:

   - how it feels to set out on an adventure.
   - finding out a friend has done something illegal.
   - a difficult choice you had to make.

5. The Old West has been the subject of many movies and television shows. In what ways is it pictured in *Lonesome Dove* that is different from most westerns you've seen? Are the cowboys described in *Lonesome Dove* similar to the cowboys portrayed by John Wayne? You might want to look at Westerns from different periods on television or video. Write

down your thoughts about the differences between them.

6. If you could talk to Larry McMurtry, what questions would you ask about his writing? You might want to write the questions in your journal.

About Larry McMurtry

✲

Readers of *Lonesome Dove* will not be surprised to learn that Larry McMurtry is the son and grandson of Texas ranchers. He was born in 1936 in Wichita Falls, Texas, a small town that was the model for one of his most famous books, *The Last Picture Show*. This book was made into a movie starring Cybill Shepherd, Timothy Bottoms and Jeff Bridges.

McMurtry grew up on his family's ranch. Although he had been riding horses since the age of three, McMurtry preferred reading books and writing to being a rancher. He graduated from North Texas State University in 1958 and later received a master's degree from Stanford University in California.

McMurtry has written several books about his native Texas. One of the most well known is *Terms of Endearment*, about a forty-nine-year-old widow who tries to dominate her daughter's life. In 1983, this book was made into a very popular movie starring Shirley MacLaine, Debra Winger and Jack Nicholson.

Larry McMurtry was awarded the Pulitzer prize for *Lonesome Dove*, which was published in 1985. The Pulitzer is one of the most prestigious awards for a novel. His next book was *Anything for Billy*, a novel about Billy the Kid, the famous outlaw. McMurtry's most recent book is *Some Can Whistle*, which is set in modern-day Texas.

McMurtry grew up when much of the American frontier had already vanished. But he enjoyed listening to his grandfather's stories about cowboys, cattlemen and life on the lonely plains of the Old West. In an article about Texas, he wrote: "A part of my generation may keep something of the frontier spirit even though the frontier is lost." In books like *Lonesome Dove*, McMurtry keeps this frontier spirit alive for future generations.

LONESOME DOVE: The Miniseries

In 1985, many entertainment executives felt that Americans weren't interested anymore in movies about the Old West. But Suzanne de Passe, the New York–born president of Motown Productions, believed in *Lonesome Dove*. She fought to get the book made into a television miniseries. Her instincts were correct. *Lonesome Dove* was one of the most popular television programs in history.

Lonesome Dove appeared on CBS in February 1989. It was eight hours long, shown over four evenings.

Robert Duvall played the Gus McCrae character. Tommy Lee Jones played Woodrow Call. The part of Jake Spoon was played by Robert Urich. Ricky Schroeder played Newt, and Danny Glover played Deets. Other stars included Anjelica Huston and Diane Lane.

The miniseries of *Lonesome Dove* was one of the most expensive television programs ever made. The total cost was $16 million. Most of the money was spent trying to make the movie as authentic as possible. Old photographs of the frontier were studied to make sure that each costume was historically accurate. It took three months to film *Lonesome Dove*. The movie was shot in Texas and New Mexico.

Viewers liked the *Lonesome Dove* miniseries, and so did the critics. The reviewer for *Newsweek* magazine called it "a genuine triumph." It was rerun in 1991.

About the Old West

*

Lonesome Dove takes place in the American West during the 19th century, an age of pioneers, cowboys, Indians and buffalo.

The early British settlers in America in the 1600s and 1700s stayed close to the Atlantic Ocean, which was their lifeline to supplies from England and other parts of Europe. But as the number of settlers increased, they needed to search for new farmland. They started to move inland, pushing the frontier, the outer edge of land that was settled, farther and farther west. This movement started slowly but began to pick up steam in the 19th century as more and more people left their homes in the East for greater opportunities in the West. They settled in territories that have now become states, such as Oklahoma, Montana, Texas and California.

In 1849, when gold was discovered in California, people rushed to that state by the thousands. By the early 1890s, there was no longer an American frontier.

The American Indian

Before the first British settlers arrived in the 1600s in what is now called North America, the only inhabitants of this land were Native Americans, often called Indians.

Indians had lived in North America for many thousands of years. They inhabited all parts of the continent, and were divided into many tribes, each with its own customs, laws and language.

Many Indians lived on the land between the Mississippi River and the Rocky Mountains. This area is called the Great Plains. The Indians of the Great Plains hunted buffalo, which they used for food and clothing. The buffalo moved from place to place on the Great Plains. The Indians also moved around, following the buffalo.

White men began to move to the Great Plains in the 1800s to start wheat farms. These settlers wanted the Indians to stay in one place. But the Indians wanted to continue to move about the Great Plains hunting buffalo. There were many bloody wars between Indians and white men. Many settlers were killed. But many more Indians were killed. The Indians were forced to sign treaties that gave away their rights to the lands their ancestors had lived on for thousands of years. By 1887, most Indians had been forced to move to territories set aside for them, called reservations. They could no longer roam the Great Plains hunting buffalo.

Pioneers and Cowboys

Americans who left their homes and moved west were called pioneers. They took their belongings with them in covered wagons, and used horses and oxen to pull these wagons.

Some of these pioneers settled on the large prairies of the American West. Prairies are areas of rolling hills covered with wild grass. They are ideal for raising cattle. The cattle ranches of the Old West supplied the meat for the cities of the eastern parts of the United States.

Men who became experts at handling cattle were known as cowboys. They mastered the skills needed to control large herds of cattle. These skills included riding a horse and roping cows. Cowboys would work for the cattle owners on the ranch and move the cattle when they traveled to market.

The easiest way to control a large number of cattle was in big groups, called herds. Most herds contained about 2,500 cattle. It took eight to twelve cowboys to manage such a herd. In the fall, cowboys rounded up the cattle, including some cows that had no owner and were roaming the prairie. They branded these cattle with their own symbol to show that they were the owners. All winter they kept watch over the herd, making sure that thieves didn't take any of their cattle. In the spring they chose the cattle ready for the market and moved these animals to the nearest railroad town, often hundreds of miles away. Once the cattle were sold, cowboys enjoyed a brief period of relaxation before returning home.

By the end of the 1800s, most cowboys had been forced to settle on ranches. Ranches had barbed-wire fences and were usually close to a railway. The skills of the cowboy were not needed on these ranches. The days of the cowboy were over.

Texas Rangers

Another important figure of the Old West was the Texas Ranger. Today, Texas is America's second-largest state, with big cities such as Houston and Dallas. Back in the frontier days, Texas was a wild and sometimes lawless place.

To bring law and order to the area, a group of cowboys formed a military force and called themselves Texas Rangers. They were paid by settlers in Texas to protect them from Indian attacks. Later, the Texas Rangers served as a border patrol between Mexico and the United States.

The Texas Rangers were known for their independent spirit. They provided their own horses and guns. They refused to wear uniforms or salute their officers. They were also known for their shooting skills and their bravery. The Texas Rangers' favorite weapon was the six-shooter.

By the 1870s, the Texas Rangers had brought law and order to the Texas frontier. Shortly after that, their skills were not called on as often. Like the cowboy, the Texas Ranger began to fade into history.

The Old West in America's Memory

The West still has cattle and wide-open spaces, but it no longer exists as the Native Americans and early settlers knew it. Most of America has been settled. The telephone, the television, the car, and the airplane have made this country seem like a much smaller place than it was when the cowboy and the Texas Ranger rode in the saddle.

But the Old West lives on in the imagination of the American people and people around the world. Movies about the frontier, called westerns, have kept the legends of the cowboy alive for all Americans. These movies, with actors like John Wayne and Gary Cooper, made the cowboy into an American hero, a symbol of the country's spirit. Unfortunately, these movies misrepresented the Native American as violent and dishonest.

As America has become more and more civilized, the Old West continues to fascinate Americans. One of the most popular movies in recent years was *Dances With Wolves*, a film about the frontier that showed the Native American in a positive light. *Lonesome Dove* was a bestselling novel and became a television miniseries watched by millions of people around the world.